Disney Princess

Sleeping Beauty

MOVIE CAMERA

Storybook with Film Viewer

Adapted by Judy Katschke and Olivia London
illustrated by Disney Storybook Artists

New York, New York • Montréal, Québec • Bath, United Kingdom

Long ago, in a kingdom far away, a new princess was born. Her name was Aurora, and she had golden hair and rose lips.

The days after her birth were a joyous time for the entire kingdom. The king and queen hosted a special celebration in honor of Aurora.

During the celebration, King Stefan announced the

future joining of his kingdom with another by betrothing Princess Aurora to Prince Phillip, the son of his friend King Hubert. The two kingdoms would be joined forever with the marriage of the two kings' children.

Afterward the three good fairies—Flora, Fauna, and Merryweather—each offered the princess a gift. Flora's gift was the gift of beauty. Fauna gave Aurora the gift of song. The third fairy, Merryweather, was about to give her gift, when there was a flash of light. All of the guests at the celebration were startled. What had caused the flash of light?

Suddenly, the evil fairy Maleficent appeared, angry that she had not been invited to the celebration. "Before the sun sets on her sixteenth birthday," Maleficent declared, placing a curse on Aurora, "she shall prick her finger on the spindle of a spinning wheel and die!"

But Merryweather's gift offered hope: Aurora would not die if she pricked her finger; she would fall into a deep sleep. Only with True Love's Kiss would the spell break. Still, the king and queen were worried and sent Aurora to live in hiding with the three good fairies until her sixteenth birthday arrived. But the three fairies had to promise not to use their magic or Maleficent might find out where Aurora was hiding.

Nearly sixteen years had passed by, and the cruel Maleficent's prophecy had yet to come true. Aurora had disappeared.

"She couldn't have vanished into thin air!" Maleficent angrily yelled at her servants. "My pet," she said, turning to her raven, "you are my last hope. Circle far and wide. Search for a maid of sixteen with hair of sunshine gold and lips red as the rose. Go and do not fail me!"

Just as they had promised,

Flora, Fauna, and Merryweather had kept their magic a secret and had raised Aurora in a small cottage deep in the forest. Aurora had no idea that she was a princess or that the three fairies possessed any magic.

On the morning of Aurora's sixteenth birthday, the three fairies sent her berry picking so they could plan a celebration. They planned a party fit for a true princess. And that night, the fairies would take Aurora back to the castle so that she could meet her betrothed, Prince Phillip.

Aurora spent time with her animal friends and sang her way through the forest.

That morning, as he often did, the handsome, grown-up Prince Phillip went riding through the forest on his horse, Samson. As he rode, he heard a voice singing a lovely song.

"Do you hear that, Samson?" he asked, hearing Aurora's voice. "It's beautiful!"

Samson and Prince Phillip took off at once in search of the enchanting voice. But in his haste, Samson jumped over a small pond and accidentally dropped Prince Phillip right in the middle of it! The prince was soaked! Prince Phillip hung his cloak and hat on a tree to dry.

Aurora's animal friends came upon the cloak and hat and ran off with them. The prince yelled to them to stop, but it was too late.

Back with Aurora, the friends used the clothes to make the form of a prince, and Aurora laughed, sang, and danced dreamily.

The prince, having chased the animals, came upon Aurora and her friends. He was breathless when he saw Aurora—she was beautiful! So beautiful, in fact, that he couldn't resist dancing with her and joining in her song.

Aurora had dreamed of the handsome prince many times, and seeing him before her was a dream come true. So mesmerized were they by one another, that they sang and danced the whole morning away! Suddenly Aurora realized it was time to go.

"But when will I see you again?" the prince asked anxiously. He didn't even know his new love's name.

"This evening," Aurora answered. "At the cottage in the glen."

Back at the cottage, the fairies were having trouble getting ready for Aurora's birthday. Her new gown was unraveling at the seams, and her seventeen-layer cake was oozing onto the floor. The fairies realized that if they wanted a special celebration, they would need to use magic.

As they worked, sparks from their wands traveled up the chimney. Maleficent's raven, who was still searching for Aurora, spotted the magical sparks immediately!

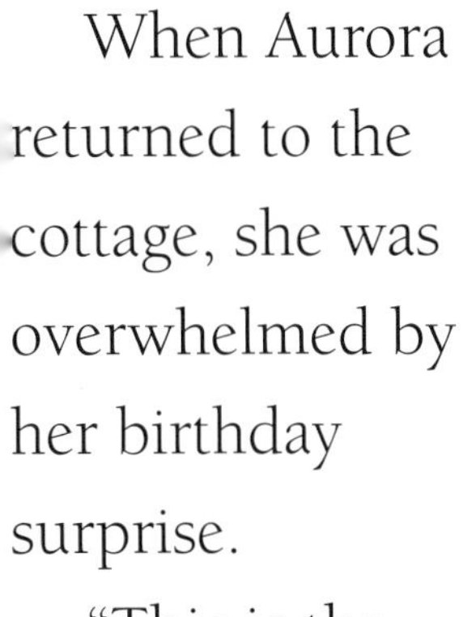

When Aurora returned to the cottage, she was overwhelmed by her birthday surprise.

"This is the happiest day of my life!" she cried joyfully. "Just wait till you meet him."

"You met some stranger?" they asked, worried.

"He's not a stranger," she told them. "We've met before...once upon a dream."

Right then and there, the fairies became sure of one thing—Aurora was in love!

"You are already betrothed," they told her regretfully, "to Prince Phillip, dear."

"But that's impossible," Aurora told them. "To marry a prince, I'd have to be a—"

"A princess!" the three fairies confirmed. "Princess Aurora. Tonight we are taking you back to your father."

When Aurora told them that her love was coming to the cottage that evening, they remarked gravely that she could never see the young man again. And so, that evening, with a heavy heart, Princess Aurora went with the three fairies through the forest to the castle in silence.

Little did they know that the raven had heard every word they had said, and very soon, so would Maleficent!

When Maleficent heard that Aurora had returned, she set off to make her prophecy come true. With her magical powers, she entered Aurora's castle chamber unseen by the three fairies. Maleficent lured Aurora down a dark magical passageway, at the end of which stood a solitary spinning wheel.

"Touch the spindle! Touch it, I say!" the evil voice commanded her.

As if under a spell, Aurora placed her finger on the tip of the spindle and fell to the ground in a deep sleep. By the time the good fairies arrived, it was too late.

"You poor simple fools!" Maleficent growled at the three fairies. "Thinking you could defeat me, the mistress of all evil!"

Upset, the fairies planned a spell to put the kingdom to sleep, too.

As she worked, Flora overheard King Hubert confide that Prince Phillip was in love with a peasant girl he had met "once upon a dream"! Prince Phillip was Aurora's true love—he could break the spell!

But once again, the fairies were too late! Maleficent had already captured him and had locked him deep in the dungeons atop the Forbidden Mountains.

With good magic on their side, the fairies freed the prince. They

ffered him a magical Shield of Virtue and a Sword of Truth to protect him in battle. Knowing now that Princess Aurora was in fact his true love, Prince Phillip fought Maleficent fiercely all the way down the Forbidden Mountain and up to the castle.

Maleficent transformed herself into a powerful dragon, breathing fiery flames everywhere. But with help from the fairies and his Sword of Truth, Prince Phillip killed the dragon at last, and Maleficent was gone forever.

Finally, Prince Phillip climbed the castle steps and bestowed upon Sleeping Beauty True Love's Kiss! The good fairies lifted the sleeping spell from the kingdom, and everyone rejoiced in Princess Aurora's safe return.

As she and her beloved prince began to dance, their fathers celebrated the union of their two children—and kingdoms.

But none rejoiced in this happy ending quite as much as Aurora and Prince Phillip!